BATMAN BEYOND

No Place Like Home

Written by Sholly Fisch

Based on the comic-book story
by Hillary J. Bader

Illustrated by John Delaney
and Dave Cooper

Batman created by Bob Kane

Random House New York

A Random House PICTUREBACK® book.

Published in the United States by Random House, Inc., New York, and simultaneously in Canada
by Random House of Canada Limited, Toronto. Library of Congress Catalog Card Number: 00-100884
ISBN 0-375-80652-0

www.randomhouse.com/kids www.dccomics.com

Printed in the United States of America
October 2000 10

This is Gotham City in the future.
Deep underground, there are tunnels that carry pipes, wires...
...and Batman.
These tunnels go on forever!
Hey, Mr. Wayne, are you sure I'm going the right way?

The map says you're doing fine.
That's easy for you to say. You get to sit home and watch the whole thing on TV.
Meanwhile, I'm down in these creepy tunnels!
Sorry. It's the easiest way to sneak into the Plastino factory.
And you've got to get there before Blight does.

Yeah, I know. If Blight steals the zeliconium from the factory...
...he'll blow up the whole city.

Well, I'll be there soon.
Ugh!
This door could use a little—
SKREEEEEEK!
don't believe it!

Who are you?

I don't know
how you found us...
...but I won't
let you hurt us!
Huh?

Who said anything
about hurting you?
Hurt you?

I mean, you're the one waving sticks around...
Hold on, Akira! Don't you know who that is?
It's the **Batman**!

Can I touch your wings?
Are you really Batman?
Batman!
Do you have gum?
I don't know, Virginia...
Relax, Akira. It's fine.
How can you be so sure?
Because they're sure.
And they're never wrong.

Quickly, Batman tells them about his mission.
...and that's why I'm here. Now it's your turn to explain.
Not now. You need to move fast.
Come on. Annie knows every shortcut through these tunnels.
We'll talk on the way

So what are you kids doing in these tunnels, anyway?
We live here.
You live here?! Don't you have homes—families?
Not the kind you mean. We're orphans.
But—who takes care of you all?
We take care of each other.

Sounds hard.
I still miss my dad sometimes.
Yeah. I know how you feel.
But it's not so bad. I've got a new family now.
That's righ And nothing going to pu us apart.

Soon—
There.
The factory's just up those stairs.
Wait.
If anyone knew that we live in the tunnels, they'd split us up and send us away.
Promise not to tell anyone about us.
Okay. I promise.

You'd better head back now. Blight's dangerous. From here on...

...I'm going alone.

The Plastino factory. It's show time.

This should be it. I guess I got here first.
Danger:
Keep Out!
Guess again.
Blight!

You'll never get in my way again!
Well, I wouldn't say "never"...
Aaaaah!

Oof! Thanks for the lift, Batman.
Now I have the zeliconium!
When I open this tube—
FSSSSSSSST
What—?

What did you do?!

Just a little casium spray. It turns dangerous zeliconium into plain old rock.

No!
You've ruined everything!

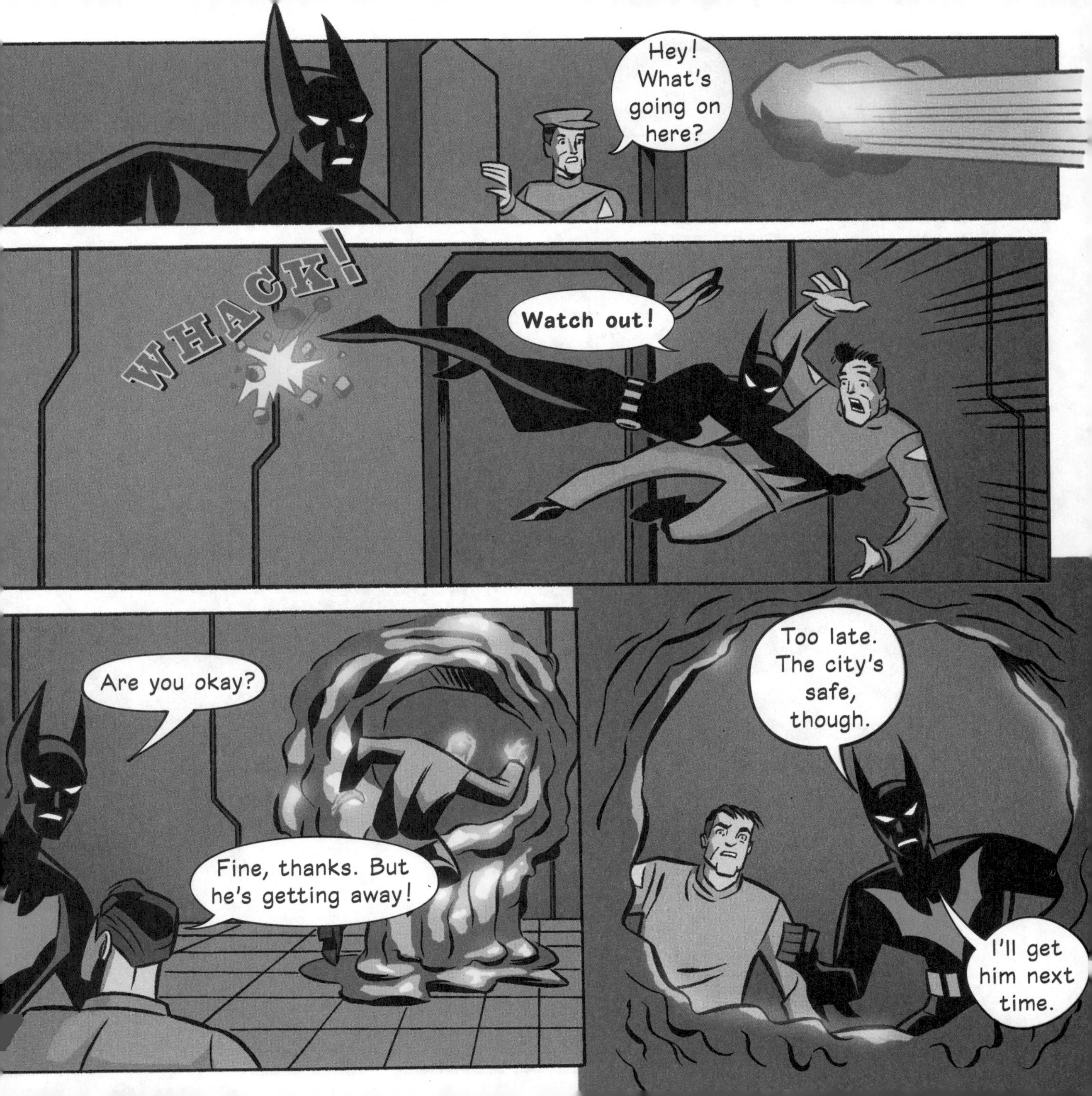
Hey! What's going on here?
WHACK!
Watch out!
Are you okay?
Fine, thanks. But he's getting away!
Too late. The city's safe, though.
I'll get him next time.

All of the tests show that the zeliconium is harmless now. Nice job.
That leaves just one bit of unfinished business.
What are you going to do about those kids in the tunnel?

What does Batman always do when people need help?
I'll help them.

TOYS
ESTI'S PETS

So? What do you say now, Akira?
Okay. You were right.
Yes, Virginia...

...there is a Batman.

GREYSCALE

BIN TRAVELER FORM

Cut By JOHN TIRADO Qty 30 Date 07/76/2024

Scanned By____________________ Qty__________ Date____________

Scanned Batch IDs

_______________ _______________ _______________

Notes / Exception

____

____

____

____

____